"ICONIC" - AUNT SOPHIE HARPO (KID CRUSADER VS. THE YUPPIE)

"GABBY METZLER IS ONE OF THE BEST COMICS WRITERS COMING UP."
-KEVIN ECKERT (DETROIT COMIX PARTY)

"GABBY METZLER BRINGS US INTO BECKY'S WORLD IN FAT GIRL LOVE CLUB THROUGH EXPRESSIVE DRAWINGS AND DEPICTIONS OF HIGH SCHOOL PAIN THAT FEEL HONEST AND ALL-TOO-FAMILIAR."
-EMI GENNIS (THE PLUNGE)

"FAT GIRL LOVE CLUB IS POIGNANT AND HILARIOUS IN EQUAL PARTS. WITH EACH NEW ISSUE GABBY METZLER BUILDS AN ABSORBING STORY ACTED BY CHARACTERS THAT DON'T OFTEN SIT IN THE PUBLIC EYE."
-LAUREN MCCALLISTER (TEEN GIRL KILLED)

INTIMATE, FRIGHTENING, INNOVATIVE AND FAMILIAR ALL AT THE SAME TIME! THE FAT GIRL LOVE CLUB IS AN AMAZING BOOK!
-JEFF SMITH (BONE)

WINNER OF THE *CXC* EMERGING ARTIST AWARD 2020

BROUGHT TO YOU, THANKS TO A GRANT, FROM THE GREATER COLUMBUS ARTS COUNCIL

Greater Columbus
Arts Council

CHAPTER 1: 2ND PLACE SPACE PRIZE FOR COMICS

CHAPTER 4: WINNER OF THE SPACE PRIZE FOR COMICS

AUTHOR'S NOTE

   NOT A LOT OF PEOPLE LISTEN TO TEENS LIKE THE
ONES IN THIS STORY. THEY'RE TERRIBLE AT TALKING, BUT
STILL! THERE'S THIS NOTION AROUND THAT KIDS DON'T
HAVE REAL PROBLEMS, AS IF MOST MENTAL ILLNESSES
DON'T ARISE IN YOUR TEENS. THERE'S A POPULAR PODCAST
THAT ENDS EVER EPISODE SAYING SOMETHING LIKE, "IT'S
EMBARASSING TO BE A KID BUT AT LEAST WE *ALL*
SURVIVED." *FUCK THAT.* BEING A KID IS BEING A PERSON
AND SOME KIDS DON'T SURVIVE. WE ALL KNOW PEOPLE
WHO DIDN'T OR ALMOST DIDN'T MAKE IT TO 20. YOUNG
PEOPLE ARE UP AGAINST EVERYTHING IN LIFE FOR THE
FIRST TIME. THEY HAVE SO FEW TOOLS. WRITING STORIES
LIKE THIS HAS BEEN A TOOL FOR ME. I HOPE THE STORY
WILL SHOW THAT THERE ARE TOOLS THAT MAKE LIFE NOT
ONLY BEARABLE, BUT RICH.

   ON TOP OF THAT LOFTY GOAL, THIS IS A BOOK
ABOUT FAT PEOPLE NAVIGATING LOVE. HINT - IT'S LIKE
EVERYONE ELSE - HORRIBLY AT FIRST AND THEN BETTER
OVER TIME.

IN FAT GIRL LOVE,
GABBY METZLER

FOR JOSH

I WISH YOU WERE STILL HERE

ACKNOWLEDGEMENTS

I AM SO GRATEFUL FOR: JOSH, JOSH (TWO REAL JOSH'S), APRIL, MOM,
OLIVIA, MCKAYLA, FONZIE, RACHEL, LAUREN, MIKE, CAITLYN, ARI,
JILLIAN, MARIAH, JONATHAN, AMELIA, RENEE, ALEX, CALEB, ALLI,
PAIGE, DIANE, EMMA, CHEYENNE. RACHEL AND CATHY

THE FAT GIRL LOVE CLUB

BY GABBY METZLER

THE FOUNDER

CHAPTER 1

IN OHIO, IN 2010 A CERTAIN MONSTROUS STATUE OF JESUS WAS STRUCK BY LIGHTENING.

AND BURNED OFF ITS APERTURE.

IT'S MOST LIKELY THE ASHES FELL ON THE GROUNDS OF THE STATUE'S MEGA CHURCH.

THE NEIGHBORING COLOSSAL FLEA MARKET,

THE STATE PRISON,

THE LUXURY OUTLET MALL.

OR EVEN ON THE CONTRUCTION SITE OF A HUGE CASINO THAT WOULD OPEN IN 2013.

CONSTRUCTION AREA
ALL TRESPASSERS
WILL BE PROSECUTED

BUT, IN THE RAIN NO ONE COULD KNOW WHERE THE ASHES FELL.

AT THE TIME OF THE FIRE, REBECCA LATRICE WAS 10 YEARS OLD.

WHEN SHE HEARD THE NEWS STORY HER HEART BROKE AND HER MIND CLOSED INTO A DEEP MOURNFUL FOCUS.

BROADCAST NEWS FOCUSED PURELY ON THE SPECTACLE OF THE EVENT.

COMMENTER'S POINTED OUT THE IRONY OF *EXODUS 20:4* "THOU SHALT NOT MAKE ANY GRAVEN IMAGE, OR ANY LIKENESS OF ANY THING THAT IS IN HEAVEN,"

 hereticinchief 11 months ago

So christians feel validated by

seeing jesus in toast but this

isn't a sign?

Read more

Reply · 7

TO THE NON BELIEVERS AND TO THE CRUEL THIS WAS A HILARIOUS END TO LOCAL EMBARRASSMENT.

Big Butter Jesus On Fire

18,229

ALONE IN HER TRAILER BECKY ONLY CONSIDERED THE ASHES. SHE REJECTED THE NEWS'S SPECTACLE. SHE CARED NOT FOR IRONY. AND WAS SPARED THE ASSAULT OF UNBELIEVERS. SHE HAD HER OWN GOAL, SHE WOULD BURY THE ASHES.

IT'S NOT AS IF THE STATUE WAS IN ANOTHER STATE. THREE TIMES A WEEK SHE AND HER MOTHER WOULD PASS ITS SKELETON, MERE MINUTES FROM THEIR BOOTH AT THE FLEA MARKET.

BECKY FIGURED IT'D TAKE A HALF HOUR TO GET TO THE MEGA CHURCH, COLLECT HER GOD, AND RETURN.

THIS WAS A PIPE-DREAM. HER MOTHER WAS WEARY OF THE WORLD AND BECKY WAS TERRIBLY AFRAID OF HER MOTHER.

SHE LET WEEKS GO BY PASSING THE REMAINS AGAIN AND AGAIN, WAITING FOR AN OPPORTUNITY

AND WHEN ONE AROSE,

SHE WAS BRAVE ENOUGH TO TAKE IT.

I THOUGHT THEY'D BE HERE.

HER SHAME GREW AS SHE SEARCHED. SHE'D WAITED TOO LONG. SHE'D GONE TO THE TOMB AND FOUND IT EMPTY. THEY HAD WASHED AWAY.

WHAT BECKY DIDN'T KNOW WAS THE STATUE HAD BEEN

MADE MOST ENTIRELY OF FIBERGLASS,

WHICH IS COMPOSED OF TOXIC RESINS AND LITTLE

SHARDS OF GLASS. THE THING IS, WHEN FIBERGLASS

BURNS IT DOESN'T SMOLDER LIKE MOST OTHER THINGS,

IT EVAPORATES.

BECKY HAD BEEN CHASING SMOKE
AND WOULD NEVER KNOW IT.

AND SHE WOULD
NEVER STOP.

FIVE YEARS LATER, IN JULY OF 2015, BECKY AND HER MOTHER STILL GO TO THE FLEA MARKET THREE TIMES A WEEK. THEY SELL SHAMPOO, BOXES OF BATTERIES, ALL MANNER OF GRANOLA BARS AND WHATEVER TRISH, BECKY'S MOTHER, CAN FIND DISCOUNTED.

THE CONSTANT RITUAL OF THEIR LIVES LULLED BECKY INTO A DISCRETE RHYTHM. SHE MAINTAINS HER DUTIES BUT IS ALWAYS SEARCHING FOR NEW WAYS TO WORSHIP HER SAVIOR WITHOUT INCITING HER MOTHER TO HER TYPICAL FITS.

BECKY DOES THE BOOTH'S GRUNT WORK, STOCKING, CLEANING, FOOT ERRANDS.

TRISH IS THE SALES TEAM. SHE CAN OCCASSIONALLY BE CHARMING BUT RECENTLY HER SALES STRATEGY INCLUDES MORE SCREAMING THAN ANYTHING ELSE.

TRISH DEEMS HERSELF A "CUT THROAT ENTREPRENEUR." THE COMMUNITY AT LARGE HASN'T ACCEPTED THIS TITLE. NONETHELESS, TRISH CARRIES ON, A BUSINESS WOMAN, A SINGLE MOTHER NO LESS, WORKING IN HARD TIMES.

SHE ASSOCIATES WITH A SMALL GROUP OF FELLOW BOOTH OWNERS. TOGETHER THEY GOSSIP, BITCH, AND STRATEGIZE TO MEET THE EVER CHANGING NEEDS OF THE FLEA MAKET. THESE ADULTS SEE TRISH AS A FRIEND. SHE SEES THEM AS FUTURE THREATS THAT MUST REMAIN PACIFIED.

YOU JUST KNOW HE'S NOT MAKING A PROFIT.

HE DOESN'T HAVE GOOD HELP. MY BECKY LOVES WORKING FOR ME.

DON'T YOU BABY?

BABY?

THESE PARENTAL AFFECTIONS ARE RESERVED FOR THE JUDGING PUBLIC EYE.

GO GET US SOME LUNCH WON'T YOU BABY? AND HURRY BACK.

YEAH. OK.

TAKE YOUR MACE AND BE EXTRA SAFE.

CAN I BUY SOMETHING FROM THE CATHOLIC BOOTH WITH THE LEFTOVER CHANGE?

QUEEN TO THE KING OF KINGS.

IT ISN'T CONSTITUTIONAL!

EXCUSE ME!!!

IN AN ATTEMPT TO REMAIN A PREDATORY FORCE IN THE FLEA MARKET TRISH HAD RESORTED TO UNETHICAL AND OFTEN TIMES ILLEGAL MEANS OF ACQUISITION.

AS A RESULT SHE'D BEEN SKIRTING SUBPOENAS AND INDICTMENTS FOR THE PAST TWO MONTHS.

COME ALONG MISS.

WAIT! WHAT ABOUT MY BABY?!?

ANGIE! WHERE YOU AT?!?

RIGHT HERE TRISHA GIRL?!?

ANGIE, WILL YOU GET BECKY HOME SAFE FOR ME?

OF COURSE TRISHA GIRL.

I'M GOING TO SUE YOUR WHOLE DEPARTMENT!

ANGIE DEVELOPED A LUMP IN HER MOUTH A COUPLE OF YEARS BACK. THE COMMUNITY PUT A GREAT DEAL OF HOPE INTO THE MUTING CAPABILITY OF THAT LUMP.

SOME CHURCH MEMBERS PLANNED TO PRAY TOGETHER THAT ANGIE WOULD BE SILENCED. WHEN THEY BEGAN TO PRAY THEY WERE HORRIFIED AT THEIR OWN CRUELTY. EVER SINCE THEY LISTEN TO ANGIE WITH HUGE SMILES ON THEIR FACES.

...ANGIE...

NICK IS REALLY JUST A PRODUCT OF YOUR GENERATION. SO DISTRACTED BY YOUR DAMN GADGETS.

ANGIE.

I'VE HEARD ON THE NEWS THAT CELL PHONES KILL YOUR BRAIN CELLS. MAKE YOU MORE STUPID EVERY MINUTE.

COULD YOU SHUT UP?!?! LIKE LONG ENOUGH THAT I COULD ASK ONE QUESTION??

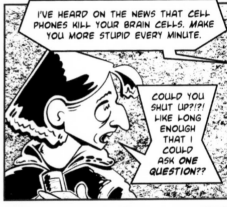

UM... WHAT AM I SUPPOSED TO DO... WHEN I GET HOME?

WELL BECKY.... WHY SHOULD I KNOW? DO WHAT YOU ALWAYS DO.

THIS IS BECKY'S HOME. THE NEIGHBORHOOD IS GOOD. MOSTLY INHABITED BY ELDERLY FOLKS, THEY'D CALL THEMSELVES CIVILLY MINDED.

THE NEIGHBORS CONSIDERED THE YOUNG DAUGHTER OF THE HOARDING WOMAN. AFTER MONTHS AND MONTHS THEY CHOSE TO CALL THE COPS RATHER THAN LIVE IN ONE OF "THOSE" TRAILER PARKS.

MOM GOT ARRESTED TODAY.

EVERYBODY SAW. SHE'LL BE REAL EMBARRASSED.

THIS IS BECKY'S BLOG. SHE'S GAINED POPULARITY AS A FANFITION AUTHOR. HER WORK CHRONICLES MARY MAGDALENE AND JESUS' INTIMATE LIFE IN A MULTIVERSE OF LICENTIOUS POTENTIAL.

Anonymous said:
That was the most perverted thing I've ever read i hope you get the help you need

Anonymous said:
Could you do an AU where Jesus and Vishnu fuck?

THIS IS GRANDPA TIM.
TRISH ALWAYS SAID HE
WAS STRICT ABOUT
EVERYTHING EXCEPT SIN.

ROUGH DAY
RIGHT?

YEAH.

LET ME COME
IN BABY

BACK WHEN BECKY WAS AROUND 8 YEARS
OLD, GRANDPA TIM MADE AN ATTEMPT TO
RECONNECT WITH HIS ONLY FAMILY.

JESUS.

THAT YEAR HE TOOK BECKY AND TRISH OUT
TO WEEKLY DINNERS. EACH RESTAURANT
BECAME A VENUE FOR TRISH TO VERBALLY
BATTLE THE OLD MAN. TERRIFIED, BECKY
SECRETLY ASKED HIM TO STOP CALLING.

I CAN'T BELIEVE YOUR MOTHER
MAKES YOU LIVE LIKE THIS.

SHE LIVES
HERE TOO.

I THOUGHT I'D SIT YOU
DOWN, BUT THERE'S NO
WHERE TO SIT... SO.

I WENT AND TALKED TO
YOUR MOM AND OFFICER
O'NEIL AND THE LITTLE
WOMAN WHO SITS
AT THE DESK.

YOUR MOM STOLE $200
MORE THAN THE LIMIT
THAT RAISES HER BAIL
FROM AN AMOUNT WE
CAN AFFORD TO ONE..
WE CAN'T.

IT'S BEEN JUST ME HERE, FOR UH, A GOOD WHILE.

THIS IS YOUR ROOM. IT'S EVEN DECORATED FOR A LADY FROM WHEN MY MOTHER LIVED HERE.

SHE DIDN'T DIE HERE DID SHE?

NOT TECHNICALLY. HA!

...I BETTER LEAVE YOU ALONE.

THE INITIATION

CHAPTER 2

EACH MORNING, BECKY PRAYED THAT GOD WOULD NEVER MAKE HER SPEND ANOTHER NIGHT AT GRANDPA TIM'S.

COME EAT!

GOD MUST BE TESTING BECKY'S STRENGTH.

WE BETTER HURRY UP. SHEEEWWW

COUGH!!! COUGH!!

BEING LATE WOULD MAKE YOUR MOM LOOK BAD TO THE JUDGE

TRISH HAD SAID MANY THINGS ABOUT GRANDPA TIM'S HIPOCRISY BUT NOT THIS...

BECKY HATED THE OLD STONER. HE WAS A SPECTACLE OF DEBAUCHERY. HE WAS A BLACK MARK ON HER MOTHER'S CHARACTER.

IN REALITY, THE PEOPLE IN THE COURTROOM WEREN'T LOOKING AT GRANDPA TIM. THEY WERE RIGHTFULLY ABSORBED IN THEIR OWN LIVES.

SHE HATED THE FAMILIES. THEY SHOULD BE MORE UPSET. IF THEY'RE NOT UPSET DOES THAT MEAN THEY'RE CRIMINALS TOO? HOW HAD SHE AND HER MOTHER COME TO BE SURROUNDED BY FILTH WHEN THEY'D WORKED SO HARD TO STAY PURE?

SHE HATED EVERYONE. SHE HATED THE OTHER PEOPLE ON TRIAL. THEY WERE SINNERS AND WOULD RECEIVE LESS PUNISHMENT THAN THEY DESERVED.

SHE EVEN HATED THE POLICE OFFICERS AND LAWYERS WHO WERE EITHER FOOLS OR CRUEL TO PERSECUTE SOMEONE AS PURE AS TRISH.

THE ONLY ONE SHE DIDN'T HATE WAS HER MOTHER.

IN NO TIME TRISH WOULD PASS THIS SPIRITUAL TEST, LORD WILLING. THEN SHE AND BECKY WOULD LIVE TOGETHER AGAIN AND THEIR BOND WOULD GROW STRONGER AND TRISH WOULDN'T THROW FITS ANY.....

THE TRIAL BEGAN QUICKLY. TWO INVESTIGATORS READ REPORTS WITH PAGE AFTER PAGE OF WHAT COULD ONLY BE LIES, STORIES OF BRIBERY, EXTORTION, DECEIT OF ALL KINDS.

THE INVESTIGATORS NAMED CERTAIN WAREHOUSES BECKY AND HER MOTHER WOULD FREQUENT. FOR SOME REASON THIS SCARED BECKY. IF THIS WAS ALL A BIG MISTAKE HOW DID THEY HAVE SO MANY DETAILS?

THEY EVEN KNEW DETAILS BECKY HAD ALMOST FORGOTTEN. LOST MEMORIES BEGAN TO DANCE IN BECKY'S MIND. EACH CRIMINAL ACCUSATION CREATING A COMPLETE NARRATIVE STRINGING TOGETHER TRISH'S LIES.

IF YOU PUT ANY OF OUR BUSINESS ON THE INTERNET I'LL BEAT YOUR BUTT!

BECKY FOUGHT THE REALIZATION. SHE COULDN'T RATIONLIZE AWAY THE ISOLATION, THE ABUSE, OR LIVING IN FILTH!

HYPOCISY LIES AND THEFT.
ALL SINS MIND YOU

3 YEARS IN PRISON WITH A CHANCE FOR PAROLE

THESE DOUBTS TOOK QUICK ROOT, RIPPING APART HER FOUNDATION UNTIL THERE WAS NO WAY SHE COULD HOLD HERSELF TOGETHER.

LET'S GET OUT OF HERE BABY-GIRL

THE INSTALLATION

CHAPTER 3

JESUS WAS HARD AT WORK CRAFTING A MISSION FOR BECKY.

LISTEN UP!!!

GOD STRUCK MY HEART AND FACE WITH HUMILITY...

JESUS CALLED BECKY TO FACE HER FEARS. SHE WOULD WORK WITH AN ENEMY TO FURTHER THE KINGDOM.

MY MIND...

HAS BEEN RACING. I KEEP FINDING MORE QUESTIONS.

LIKE, HOW DOES THIS YOUTH GROUP SHOW THE WORLD GOD'S LOVE?

HURRY GRANDPA!!!

NO ONE'S THAT HARD TO FIGURE OUT.

IF YOU STEP BACK AND LOOK AT THEM WITHIN THEIR CONTEXT.

I MEAN, EACH PERSON HAS THEIR OWN LOGIC.

IF YOU REALLY LOOK YOU CAN PREDICT SOMEONE'S ACTIONS.

THAT'S WHAT THE CONCEPT OF GOD USE TO BE. ANCIENT PEOPLE KNEW ALL ABOUT IT.

TAKE BECKY. RIGHT AWAY I CAN TELL SHE'S NAIVE.

SHE'S STRONG IN HER CONVICTIONS.

AND SHE GROWS BOUNTIFUL BANGS.

NOT FOR FASHION! NO! NO FASHION HERE...

SMACK

SHE GROWS THEM TO HIDE

YOU DON'T HAVE ME FIGURED!

THERE'S NO WAY FOR YOU TO SEE MY WHOLE LIFE STORY LIKE GOD CAN!

TELL HIM BECKY GIRL!! JOSH DON'T POUT YA HERETIC!

IT'S NOT YOUR FAULT SOMEONE ELSE DISCOVERED PSYCHOLOGY FIRST!

SKIP
SKIP

OH! HEY! WAIT!

AFTER THAT, JOSH ALWAYS FOLLOWED THE GIRLS AROUND.

GUESS HOW MANY GRAPES I CAN FIT IN MY MOUTH!

40

JOSH! STOP! EVERYONE CAN SEE!

THEY SEE THAT I'M HANDSOME.

DAD SAYS THIS IS THE BIGGEST HOME LAKE'S CONSTRUCTION HAS EVER BUILT.

I HID THE BOOZE IN HERE.

MY UNCLE'S APPRENTICE SAYS HE CAN GET US ANY BOOZE WE WANT NOT JUST THESE.

HA! WAIT!

NOW YOU CAN REALLY KILL HER.

RUDE!

...NOW A KIND CARPENTER ...U SHOULD GET TO ...OW ASSHOLE!

UGH! ALL YOU EVER TALK ABOUT IS JESUS

IF YOU WANNA TALK LET'S GET REAL BECKY. YOU BELIEVE IN A BOOK, AN ANTHOLOGY REALLY, WRITTEN BY DOZENS OF GUYS, THAT WE KNOW NOTHING ABOUT HISTORICALLY.

HOW CAN YOU TAKE YOURSELF SERIOUSLY!?!

YOU KIDS BETTER GET READY FOR YOUR DANCE.

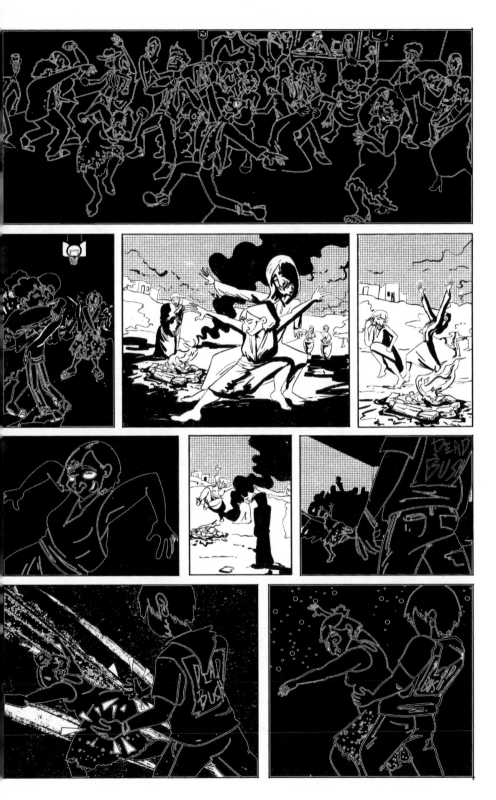

SLAP   SLAP

SLAM!

SKRRR.

BARRICADE!

HE WAS CUTE FOR A NASTY BOY.

HE'S A PREDATORY INCEL CUCK LOSER.

WHAT MADE HIM THINK I'D WANT TO DANCE WITH HIM LIKE THAT? I'M NOT A SLUT. I DON'T WEAR MAKEUP OR ANYTHING.

WELL... I DIDN'T KNOW YOU FELT THAT WAY ABOUT... MAKEUP.

BANGS HE DOESN'T CARE WHAT YOU WANT.

THIS IS PUNISHMENT FOR FALLING FROM GRACE AT HANGING OUT WITH SINNERS.

THE GRAND ORDER

CHAPTER 4

DON'T CROSS THE YELLOW LINE!

WOOOOO

I THINK I PEED THE GUY IN THE OTHER CAR'S PANTS.

WOW. I DIDN'T KNOW THERE WERE NEIGHBORHOODS LIKE THIS IN CIRCLEVILLE.

I WISH I GREW UP HERE I COULD HAVE PLAYED WITH OTHER KIDS.

THERE WERE KIDS IN YOUR TRAILER PARK.

MOM SAID THAT OUR PARK WAS TRASH AND I HAD TO RISE ABOVE.

GOD THAT GIRL. YOUR NEIGHBORHOOD WAS GOOD, ER, RELATIVELY.

TURN HERE I'LL SHOW YOU A TRASHY NEIGHBORHOOD

THE VIBE COULD USE SOME WORK!

ONE OF MY OLD BUDDIES FROM THE PLUMBER'S UNION WAS STABBED IN THAT WHITE HOUSE OVER THERE. HE WAS AMAZING AT HIS JOB. ONE TIME I SAW HIM PEE IN A MASON JAR AND DRINK IT WHEN HE THOUGHT I WASN'T LOOKING

IS THAT A FIGHT OVER THERE?

GOSH I WISH WE COULD WATCH IT.

WISH! WISH! I SAID WISH.

DON'T STOP! WE'RE GONNA GET SHOT!!!

SCREECH!!

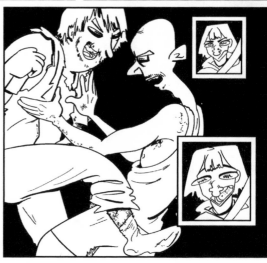

IF YOUR BROTHER SINS AGAINST YOU 40 TIMES AND COMES FOR FORGIVENESS. FORGIVE HIM 40 TIMES 40.

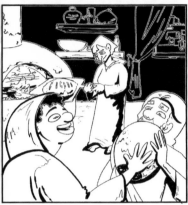

THIS IS THE BIGGEST CROWD HE'S EVER HAD WHAT IF THEY HATE WHAT HE SAYS? WHAT IF THEY REVOLT?!?

OR WORSE WHAT IF THEY LAUGH AT HIM AND WE'RE THE ONLY ONES WHO BELIEVE WHAT HE SAYS?

AFTER ALL THIS TIME YOU STILL DOUBT. HOW? LOOK AT ALL THESE PEOPLE.

I BELIEVE IN HIS WORDS. I SAID THEM FIRST BUT BETTER.

EVEN IF WE'RE THE ONLY ONES WHO BELIEVE HIM IT'S BECAUSE WE'RE CLOSE ENOUGH TO SEE THE GOOD IN HIM.

LOVE IS FOCUSING ON SOMEONE'S BEST.

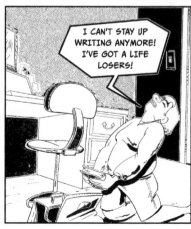

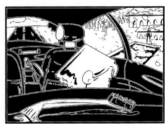

TSK. TSK.

DID I HEAR RIGHT? JEN IS SPENDING A WEEK IN D.C?

YES! SHE WON SEVERAL GRANTS FOR HER YOUTH INITIATIVE.

SHE'LL BE ABLE TO GET INTO ANY COLLEGE SHE WANTS. HAS BECKY BEEN PULLING HER WEIGHT IN THE FUNDRAISER?

OH GOSH TRISH, I'VE BEEN MEANING TO TELL YOU.

CHURCH. WE'RE GOING TO CHURCH... THAT'S SO BEYOND FINE. I SPENT MY WHOLE LIFE IN CHURCH. I'M GOOD AT CHURCH.

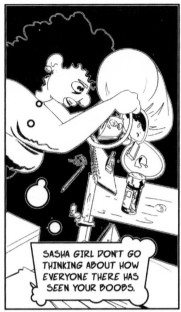

SASHA GIRL DON'T GO THINKING ABOUT HOW EVERYONE THERE HAS SEEN YOUR BOOBS.

AT LEAST I'VE LOST LIKE 30 POUNDS ON THESE PILLS.

WHERE IS THAT BOY?!?

HERE.

THAT'S FINE JOSH MOST PEOPLE DON'T SAY I'M SORRY FOR MAKING YOU LATE.

SHIT ALMOST FORGOT TO TAKE MY SKINNY PILL.

BECKY HAD TO DO SOME NEGOTIATING TO FREE UP HER WEDNESDAY NIGHTS.

YOU GUYS DIDN'T HAVE TO COME WITH ME.

I DID SO! I'M NOT GONNA HAVE JEN PULLING ANY OF HER BULLSHIT ON YOU. NOT ALL BY YOURSELF.

WE JUST NEED TO ACT CALM AND GET THROUGH THE BIBLE STORY AND THE GOSSIPY PRAYERS WITHOUT LOSING IT.

THAT WEED IS GOOD ENOUGH TO MAKE ME ENJOY ANY BIBLE STORY.

I HOPE IT'S ONE OF THOSE BIBLE STORIES WITH A LOT OF RAPE AND WAR.

JOSHY BOY I'VE BEEN THINKING THAT IF WE STOP TELLING WAR STORIES THERE WILL STOP BEING ANY WARS.

GIRL I CAN'T DEAL WITH YOU AND JEN! GET A TOLERANCE!!!

FUCK! IT'S COLD. WASN'T IT LIKE 70 DEGREES YESTERDAY.

WHAT ARE YOU, NEW TO OHIO?

JOSH AND SASHA SAID THAT THEY COULD HANDLE YOUTH GROUP MORE IF THEY STOWED AWAY AFTERWWARD IN ORDER TO PLAY IN THE GYM *AT NIGHT* THEY DIDN'T KNOW ABOUT JEN AND EDITH'S WEEKLY PROCESSING SESSIONS. IT SEEMS THE EMOTIONAL TOLL ON A SELF APPOINTED SPIRITUAL LEADER IS IMMENSE.

WAIT!

THEY'RE GONE. THE LIGHT'S OUT.

HEY LOOK, BUTT SCOOTERS!

WOOOAAA!

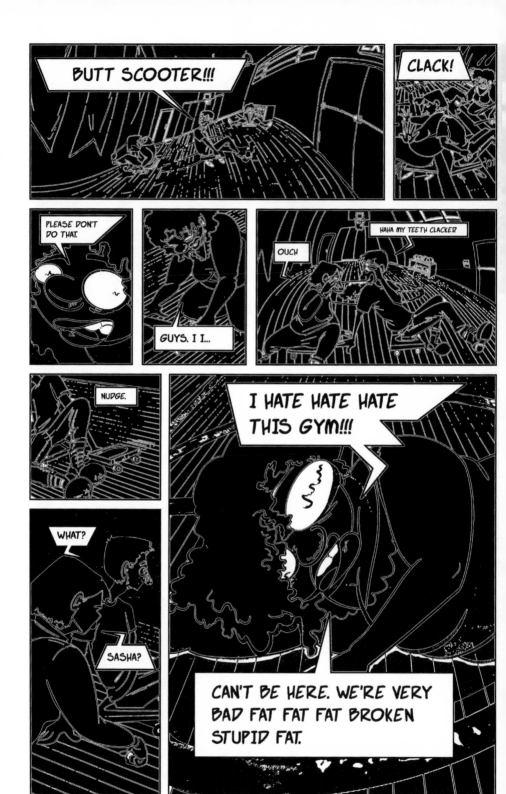

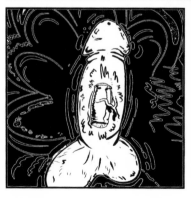

A WHILE BACK, GRANDPA TIM MENTIONED TO BECKY THAT HIS HEART USED TO GIVE HIM FITS BEFORE HE RETIRED. HE SAID IT CASUALLY SO, BECKY TOOK IT CASUALLY.

SHE'D NEVER HAD TO SIGN SOMEONE INTO ANYTHING, MUCH LESS A HOSPITAL.

HUFF HUFF MY FRIEND JUST TOOK MY GRANDPA INTO THE BACK... HUFF HUFF

WHAT'S YOUR MEDICAL EMERGENCY?

PROTECTION REPELS FROM ME. SYNTHETIC GIRL MADE FROM FOREVER FROZEN FOOD POSTPONED DEATH FOR LIFE.

ARE YOU ABLE TO SIT QUIETLY IN A CHAIR SYNTHETIC GIRL?

YES.

FILL IT OUT.

WE'RE NOT THE ONLY DOOMED KIDS. WE'RE A SYMPTOM. LAST CHOSEN. SET APART.

WE'RE NOT DOOMED SWEETIE.

YOU'RE THAT PRUDE FROM THE DANCE.

YOUR GINGER BOY ISN'T HERE.

WHAT'S YOUR FRIEND SO HIGH ON?

SHE'S NOT HIGH. SHE'S WORRIED BECAUSE SHE'S CAPABLE OF THINKING ABOUT OTHER PEOPLE.

HIGH GIRL, YOU WANNA SEE IF I CAN READ YOUR MIND? I USUALLY CAN IF I'M HIGH ENOUGH.

NO! SO LYING ABOUT CRAZY SHIT IS HOW YOU GET GIRLS?

CRAZY SHIT IS TRUE SOMETIMES. LOOK, WIDE EYES, I KNOW YOU'RE SCARED OF THOSE COPS OVER THERE.

STREET BOY SEES THE LAYERS. HE KNOWS THE ROADS. HE'S LAUGHING AT US LOOKING AT OUR MAPS. HE CAN HEAR OUR NAIVE QUESTIONS.

YOU KNOW WHAT ELSE I HEAR? I HEAR HOW SICK YOUR THOUGHTS ARE. WE BURY OUR SICKEST THOUGHTS SO DEEP THAT THEY BECOME OUR FOUNDATION.

THIS IS CRAZY TALK..

I KNOW YOU BELIEVE ME. YOU'RE MEETING THE CRACKS UNDER YOUR MIND YOU'VE DISTURBED THEM. NOW THEY'RE SHIFTING.

THERE'S NO WAY TO ENJOY AN EARTHQUAKE, LITTLE CASUALTY. WELCOME TO DESTRUCTION

ALWAYS LOOKED AT, NEVER SEEN!

BITE
BITE
BITE

REBECCA?

YOUR GRANDPA'S GOING TO BE JUST FINE. WE PUT A STENT IN. HE SHOULD BE READY TO PICK UP IN A FEW DAYS.

SASHA WAS SITTING ON THE HOOD OF THE CHEROKEE LIKE A GOOD GIRL. SO WE'RE BREATHING AND COUNTING TO TEN.

AWESOME. UH. GREAT. GRANDPA TIM IS FINE. WE CAN GET HIM IN TWO DAYS.

GUYS... WE HAVE TO QUIT DRUGS. HAVE TO, HAVE TO. DARKNESS IS ALL AROUND WE LET IT IN.

LET'S TALK ABOUT THAT WHEN YOU'RE FEELING BETTER. K?

NO! I WON'T FEEL SO STRONGLY ABOUT IT LATER. WE HAVE TO AGREE NOW!

I WANT TO QUIT TOO. IT'S LIKE YOU SAID BEFORE. I CAN'T JUSTIFY WEED TO JESUS. WE WENT TO CHURCH HIGH. GOD'S PUNISHING US.

MAGICAL THINKING! WE HAD ONE BAD NIGHT, BANGS! JUST BECAUSE SASHA'S PARANOID DOESN'T MEAN YOU HAVE TO BE.

THIS WAS THE WORST NIGHT EVER. GOD DOESN'T WANT THIS LIFE FOR US.

FINE! IF I CAN'T CONVINCE YOU TWO WE CAN TRY AND QUIT LIKE A DRE..

THANK YOU THANK YOU JOSH! DON'T WORRY WE'LL HAVE JUST AS MUCH FUN AS BEFORE!

DRUGS AREN'T JUST...

WE'LL BE TOGETHER WITH NOTHING IN BETWEEN US.

THAT DOES SOUND NICE. WAIT. IS BOOZE A DRUG?

THE SUSPENSION

CHAPTER 5

WHIPPED CREAM CHALLENGE! GO GO GO!!!

THANKSGIVING

HMM.

UH, IT SEEMS TO ME LIKE WE INVENTED ALL INVENTIONS TO AVOID RUNNING

HEY, DO YOU GUYS WANT TO GO TO THE REC CENTER TOMORROW AND PLAY BASKETBALL OR SOMETHING?

DO YOU WANT TO DO WOODWORK? WE COULD MAKE A TABLE OR A BAR?

WHY ARE YOU YELLING AT US ABOUT MAKING A TABLE?

BECAUSE YOU'RE BORING.

PLEASE SIT DOWN AND WATCH THE DRAG QUEENS LIKE A NICE BOYFRIEND.

CHRISTMAS

AM I PRETTY?

WE'RE GONNA LOOK UP VIDEOS ON WHAT TO DO WITH THESE CHEEK BONES. YOUR JAW IS SO STRIKING.

CAN YOU SEE THE FUTURE??

I'VE JUST HAD A FLASH! THE...THE FUTURE... AI CAME UP WITH SOMETHING CALLED COMMU-TALISM. NO ONE LIKES IT.

NEW YEARS EVE

JOSH BOY I GOT TEAL SEQUINS JUST FOR YOU.

THANK YOU. I DON'T NEED ANY SPECIFIC COLOR. I'M A BIG STRONG BOY.

YOU'RE MY TASTEFUL STRONG BOY WHO I HAPPEN TO SHARE A DREAM KITCHEN PINTEREST BOARD WITH. I SEE YOU ADDING KITCHENS WITH TEAL BACK SPLASHES.

ALL WE EVER DO IS WATCH HGTV! I COULDN'T HELP BUT DEVELOP TASTE.

IF WE'RE YELLING ABOUT TV, I DON'T LIKE THE SHOW WITH THE HOARDERS AND I DON'T WANT TO GO INTO IT!

NICE JOB BABE.

PAT PAT!

IS THIS SUPPOSED TO BE ABOUT MAGIC MUSHROOMS?

YEAH THEY ATE SOME BEFORE THE COMMERCIALS.

THIS IS SO BASE LEVEL. MUSHROOMS AREN'T FOR SEEING PRETTY COLORS THEY'RE FOR HAVING MYSTICAL EXPERIENCES.

DRUGS ARE NOT MYSTICAL, THEY AREN'T DIVINE OR ANY OF THAT SHIT YOU SAY. I THINK I KNOW THAT BETTER THAN YOU DO NOW.

GOSH. THANKS FOR THE PARTY BABE. THIS HAS BEEN A BLAST BUT...

SHHHEWWWWW..

OK BLOW ONE GOD BOY.

I LIKE HANGING OUT LIKE THIS. I LIKE TALKING ABOUT REAL LIFE AND DOING LITTLE ACTIVIITIES.

ARE YOU REALLY SUCH A LITTLE PISS BABY THAT YOU THINK I'M GOING TO AGREE TO YOUR IDEAS WHEN YOU CALL ME LAZY AND BORING TO GUILT ME INTO DOING DRUGS THAT HURT ME BEFORE?

IS IT GUILT OR IS JUST HOW I FEEL!?! I CAN TALK ABOUT MY FEELINGS TOO. I'M BORED! YOU USED TO BE FUN. NOW YOU'RE NOT JUST BORING BUT ALSO PREACHY LIKE BECKY!!

OH I'M NOT LISTENING TO YOUR FEELINGS? YEAH, THAT SOUNDS LIKE ME. HAVE YOU CONSIDERED THAT WHAT YOU JUST DID WAS LIST ONE FEELING IN THE MIDDLE OF 3 ATTACKS ON ME AND ONE ON BECKY!! REALLY? THAT'S WHAT YOU THINK'S SMART ANYMORE, INSULTING BECKY OF ALL PEOPLE?!?

YOU CALLED ME A PISS BABY!!

I'M NOT WAITING AROUND FOR YOU TO HYPNOTIZE ME INTO SITTING AROUND FOR ANOTHER TWO MONTHS??? NO WAY! YOU'RE A MASTER OF GUILT, AND I'M LEAVING.

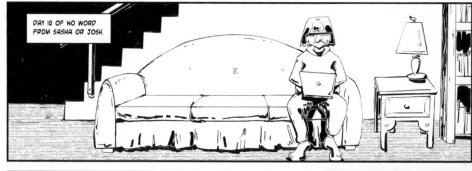

THAT'S MY PRETTY GIRL.

LOOK AT YOU... WOW LOTTA GROWING HAPPENING. ARE YOU READY FOR FREEDOM BABY?

I'VE GOT ANOTHER SURPRISE FOR YOU. YOU CAN TAKE THE TRUCK TONIGHT.

THANK YOU GRANDPA TIM! I'M GONNA GET THE GANG BACK TOGETHER.

YO SASHA! GRANDPA GAVE ME THE TRUCK TONIGHT! LET'S GO UP TO COLUMBUS OR SOMETHING!!

NO THANKS.

WHAT'S GOING ON WITH YOU? IT REALLY SEEMS LIKE YOU DON'T LIKE ME ALL OF A SUDDEN?!? AM I TOO LOUD? IS IT THE JESUS STUFF? THAT WAS JUST A JOKE?

YEAH I GUESS.

YEAH I GUESS TO WHICH PART?! THIS KINDA SEEMS LIKE BULLSHIT. YOU'RE LIKE PUNISHING ME FOR JOSH LEAVING..

BECKY WAS DRIVEN WILD. SHE COULDN'T STAND THE THOUGHT OF LOSING SASHA. SHE WAS RUNNING ON THE INSTINCT THAT HAD FUELED HER WRITING FOR YEARS. PURE LONGING. UTTER DESPERATION.

SHHUUUU

DING DONG

BARK!!!

TRIXIE GODDAMNIT HUSH UP! TANK TANK TANK COME ON!!!!

BARK!!!

BARK!!!

HOW THE FUCK DID YOU FIND MY HOUSE?

I... I... KNOW THE NEIGHBORHOOD.

HUH HUH HUH.

SO THAT WILD EYED FREAK DOESN'T OWN YOU ANYMORE AND FIRST THING YOU DO IS COME TO MY HOUSE?

WHAT ARE THOSE? AND WHY DO YOU NEED TWO OF THEM?

FUCK COULD YOU CHILL. AND WHY DID YOU THINK I'D KNOW WHERE YOU COULD FIND MAGIC MUSHROOMS?

WHAT YOU SAID TO SASHA AT THE HOSPITAL WAS BRAGGING, DARK, MEAN BRAGGING. YOU WANTED US TO KNOW THAT WE'RE JUST PUSSIES IN THE DRUG WORLD AND YOU'VE SEEN EVERYTHING. YOU WANTED TO IMPRESS ME.

WHAT?

GURGLE GURGLE

YOU WANTED TO SCARE ME. BUT YOU DON'T SCARE ME.

BITCH, I DON'T EVEN REMEMBER THAT

WEEEZ

SO IT'S $40 FOR A SIXTEENTH

JESUS CHRIST

HELLO READER, I GOOGLED LAWS ABOUT TEENAGE SEXUALITY IN ART AND JUST GOOGLING THAT CREEPED ME OUT. I'D RATHER BE RESPONSIBLE THAN EDGY IN THIS INSTANCE. BECKY IS A SEXUAL BEING AND IS GROWING INTO A STRONGER, BOLDER PERSON WITH AGENCY TO DO DESTRUCTIVE OR HEALTHY THINGS AS SHE SEES FIT. SO... IN THIS PANEL JUST KNOW THAT UH. DRUGS ARE BEING BOUGHT, FIRST SEXUAL EXPERIENCES ARE BEING HAD. CHARACTER ARCS ARE HAPPENING.
THANKS, -GABBY

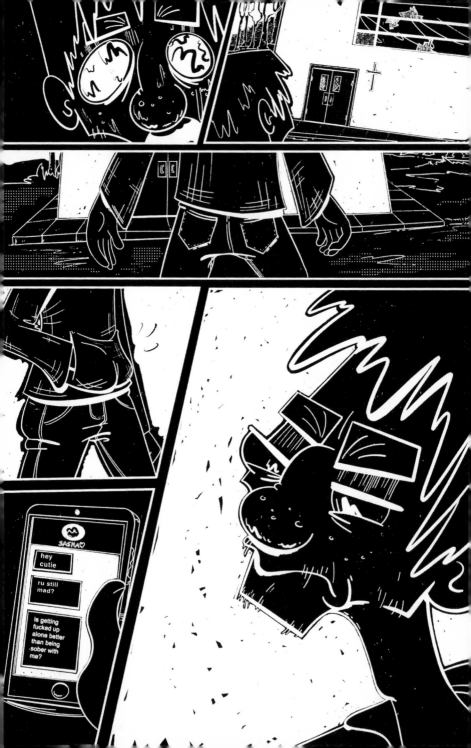

THE SUPREME APPOINTMENT

CHAPTER 6

THE NEXT MORNING.

DAMMIT BABY GET HERE.

LAST NIGHT A YOUNG WHITE MALE EXPOSED HIMSELF TO AN ELDERLY WOMAN AT CIRCLEVILLE MALL.

JOSH! WOULD JOSH DO THAT?

ARSON IS SUSPECTED IN A CIRCLEVILLE BARN FIRE SET AT MIDNIGHT LAST EVENING.

BECKY, YOU SCARY LITTLE WOMAN. WHY DID YOU HAVE TO BURN DOWN A BARN?

KNOCK! KNOCK!

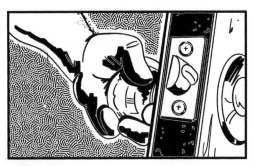

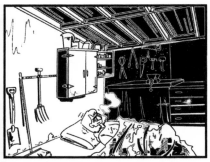

I KNOW YOU DIDN'T MAKE JOSH TRIP. HE CHOSE TO. BUT YOU GAVE HIM THE OPPORTUNITY.

THAT'S NOT WHAT LOVING JOSH LOOKS LIKE. THAT'S GIVING HIM WHAT HE WANTS BUT NOT WHAT HE NEEDS.

JOSH NEEDS AWAY FROM THIS STUFF. I CAN SEE THIS IMAGE OF HIM STAYING HERE FOREVER AND BEING SO EMPTY. I'M AFRAID FOR HIM. AND IS THAT JUST A PART OF LOVE? IS IT SOMETHING DIFFERENT? MAYBE WE HAD NO REAL CONNECTION AND DRUGS WERE THE GLUE.

I GREW UP NEXT DOOR TO YOU. WE NEVER SPOKE. WE NEVER FELT A CONNECTION.

I USED TO HEAR YOUR MOM SCREAMING... AT YOU. ALL THE TIME. AND FOR SO LONG.

I THOUGHT ONE FRIEND COULD SAVE YOU. I DON'T KNOW WHY I THOUGHT I WAS THAT POWERFUL. MAYBE IT'S ALL THIS RELIGIOUS STUFF. IT'S A HYPE MACHINE. AND LIKE I DO SEE A CHANGE. YOU'VE COME SO FAR BUT LIKE I FEEL LIKE YOU'RE A PROJECT AND I KEEP SEEING ANOTHER BROKEN PIPE AND A BUSTED WINDOW THAT WAS ALWAYS THERE. GETTING TO KNOW YOU IN LIKE THE FRAME WORK OF A PROJECT FEELS LIKE A WEIGHT. AND THAT'S MY FAULT. BUT YOU LET ME PLAY THE SAVIOR. YOU LET ME MOTHER YOU AND TEACH YOU AND CORRECT YOU. THERE'S SOMETHING THERE.

FOR A SECOND IT LOOKED LIKE JOSH SAW WHAT I LACKED THE WAY I SAW WHAT YOU LACKED.

HE TOOK ME TO HOMECOMING AND HE MADE A SHOW OF IT. THAT WAS A BIG DEAL FOR ME TO BE SEEN SO PROUDLY AND PUBLICLY LOVED.

REBECCA YOU SHOULD HELP YOUR MOTHER. WHAT KIND OF PERSON DOESN'T HELP THEIR MOTHER. SELFISHNESS IS A LIFESTYLE.

CLICK

AFTER ALL I'VE BEEN THROUGH YOU SHOULD THINK OF ME. YOU SHOULD BE WORKING TO EARN MY TRUST.

BOW TO YOUR CREATOR THE ONE WHO GIVES YOU LIFE.

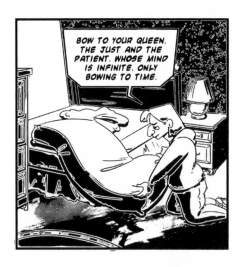

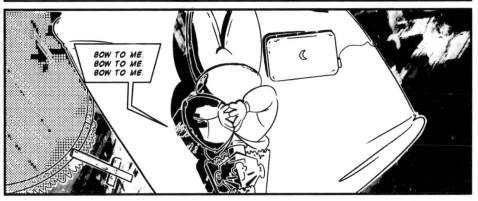

BECKY HAD LOST HER FRIENDS BUT SOMEHOW SHE SAW PAST THAT.

SHE'D CHASED HER MOTHERS LOVE AND THE FANTASY OF A GOD THAT COULD FILL HER EVERY NEED.

BUT A SEMESTER OF FRIENDSHIP HAD BEEN MORE FUFILLING THAN YEARS OF CHASING.

SHE WOULD NEVER CHASE SMOKE AGAIN. SHE WOULD BUILD FIRES.

GABBY METZLER IS A CCAD GRAD, WINNER OF THE 2020 SPACE PRIZE, AND CXC EMERGING ARTIST AWARD. SHE'S ALSO A COLORIST FOR DC'S "WHISTLE," WHICH IS REALLY COOL AND YOU SHOULD READ IT. GABBY IS A 212 RESIDENT AND HOSTS THE READING SERIES PEZTILENCE TO HONOR AND ENJOY MIDWESTERN COMICS ARTISTS. HER HOBBIES INCLUDE READING SELF-HELP BOOKS FOR OTHER PEOPLE, WATCHING BOB'S BURGERS, AND YELLING THE PHRASE "I THOUGHT I COULD CHANGE THEM!" AT DISTANT THUNDERSTORMS.

INSTAGRAM: @GABBYMETZ TWITTER: @GABBYMETZLER
WWW.GABBYMETZ.COM